Daddy Was Santa

and

other Christmas Stories

John Hope

Daddy Was Santa

and
other Christmas Stories

Daddy Was Santa, originally published 2015: Christopher discovers a secret: Daddy's Santa. But reality stops Christopher from having what he desires most.

The Drive, originally published 2015: A middle-aged man attempts to drive to his grandfather's funeral but takes an unbelievable journey instead.

Living in Illusions, originally published 2014: An unexpected visit from a Christmas angel gives Mike an opportunity to bring back his deceased father, but he realizes something he chose to forget.

Recalculating, originally published 2021: Prepared to end it all, Alister receives hopeful encouragement from an unexpected technological ally—his GPS..

Beyond the Closed Door, originally published 2021: Trevor caught Santa Claus in his hallway closet. Or is it something else?

The Visit, originally published 2020: A famed young adult author must face her greatest fear: children who remind her of her son who died much too young.

Pass It On, originally published 2016: A simple act of kindness snowballs through the lives of strangers, leading to a change of heart that stops a man from committing the ultimate sin.

ACKNOWLEDGMENTS

Thank you to the Seminole County Writers whose insightful feedback and edits were invaluable.

Contents

Story 1
Daddy Was Santa

John's Shorts
short stories - volume 2

Daddy
Was
Santa

John
Hope

I found Daddy's secret hidden in a box in the attic. Dust floated in the attic's dim light like slow-moving snowflakes above the box I had uncovered. The red top with white fluff and black round buttons rested in my hands like a stolen cookie. My insides jumped at its touch because I knew what it meant. At five years old, I knew.

I remembered when I was really little last year, Santa visited our house during a boring adult party. Daddy's pilot friends were there, standing, drinking, talking – boring, boring, boring. A bang at the door and jingling bells caused Mommy to cut the music and ordered me to the front door. I opened it to a massive, round man. He ho-ho-ho'ed and patted my head as he entered.

I sat on his lap and smelled the familiar Old Spice aftershave. He spoke, his belly jiggling, his eyes sparkling with fun.

In the attic, I smelled the suit. Old Spice and Daddy's familiar funk. I fished through the attic box and pulled out the other pieces. The soft pants, the floppy hat, and the fake beard with a looped band. I knew this had to be his. The smell. The weird-looking black buttons. Daddy had marked the box it all came in with a big red X. This was why I waited until he was gone before I dug in.

I couldn't believe I didn't figure this out before. Daddy worked a lot. He flew huge jet planes and was gone for days at a time. Now I knew where he was and what he'd been doing.

Daddy's Santa.

When he was home, getting time alone with

Daddy was hard. He'd come home and sleep in. Then he worked on the house. Then he was alone with Mommy. Then he was out at the store. Then he was doing stuff with my older sister and brother, Jenny and James – twins in high school.

I held up the costume to me. The pants were huge. They'd fit Daddy's egg-shaped body. I stepped into the pants and tossed the coat over my shoulders. They sagged over me like a deflated bear. The white cotton tickled my nose. I put the hat on my head and it covered my eyes. I grabbed the beard from the box and held it to my face, but it didn't stick. I tossed it back into the box.

I wanted to rush downstairs and show off this stuff to Mommy, Jenny, and James. Maybe they didn't know. Maybe they were just as fooled by the stories and disguise.

I shuffled along the loose attic planks to the ladder that led down the backside of the living room closet. Downstairs, I hiked up the pants, tiptoed out of the closet, and shut the door.

Mommy stepped up, her face looked dark and strained. "Oh Christ."

The sound of her let me know I shouldn't be wearing Daddy's suit. But the excitement of the truth bubbled out of me before I could stop it. "Mommy. It's Daddy's suit."

She yanked off the hat. "Take that off. We need to leave." She put her hands to her hips. "Jenny. Help Christopher get dressed."

Jenny stepped from behind Mommy. She pulled a brush through her hair, head tilted. "I'm doing my hair."

"Jenny."

Jenny sighed and rolled her eyes. She pulled my shoulder through the coat. "C'mon, Twerp."

Mommy said, "Don't forget his tie."

Jenny jerked me around, wrenching off the costume and my pajamas underneath. She was always rougher with me than Mommy, especially times like now when she seemed mad.

I asked, "When's Daddy coming home?"

She pursed her lips and pulled and pushed me harder.

"Ouch," I said, but she didn't ease up.

Pants up, buttoned up, shirt tucked, tie clipped, and shoes tied.

I felt Daddy's secret churn inside me the whole car ride. I wanted to talk to someone about it, but everyone looked too serious, too upset. Jenny had helped me out of Daddy's Santa suit, but not once did she ask where it came from. Even James, normally the one I could count on joking, just stared out the window at the passing cars. I tossed him the stuffed dog I always kept next to my car seat. He brushed it off and ignored me.

Everyone seemed to know something that I didn't. This happened a lot. Mommy would tell stuff Jenny and James and think she told everyone. And then Jenny and James told me nothing. Times like this, I always had to wait it out until I knew.

At church, we sat in the front. Lots of Daddy's pilot friends who I normally only saw at parties surrounded us. We didn't sing the church songs we normally sang. We only did one from the bulletin and sat down. Pastor Henry talked, Grandpa got up and talked, and one of Daddy's friends got up and talked. They all talked about Daddy, calling him by his name, Nick.

But no one mentioned he was Santa. I wanted to speak. I needed to tell everyone. I knew it was his secret, but I couldn't hold it in.

Pastor Henry got back up and asked everyone, "Does anyone want to say a few words about Nick?"

I leapt to my feet and waved a hand in the air and stood on my toes.

A few chuckles.

Pastor Henry said, "Okay, Christopher."

James pulled at my arm, but I shook him off and rushed to the front. I faced the crowd and spoke loud so everyone could hear. "My Daddy's Santa."

First, there was silence. Then, they all laughed, hard. They leaned into each other, and some cried.

I said, "No, really. I found his suit." I turned to Pastor Henry behind me. "He's really Santa."

He smiled and tapped my back. "Yes, yes."

No one believed me.

In the car after church, I sat arms crossed in the backseat, refusing to talk.

Jenny spoke nonstop, so fast I doubt she took a breath. James' face looked red, and he chewed his nails the way he did when he was in trouble. Jenny told James to stop, and they shoved each other until Mommy yelled.

My stomach growled when we approached IHOP. But we didn't turn into the parking lot, just kept going straight. I said, "We going to IHOP?"

"No," Mommy said.

"But we always go there after church."

"We're going somewhere else."

"Do they have pancakes?"

"No."

"But I want pancakes."

My last words flew out like nobody heard me. But I knew by Mommy's tone that repeating wouldn't make a difference. I looked out the window.

I wished Daddy was here. He'd listen to me. He'd understand.

I thought about something Pastor Henry said during church. He said, "Nick's final flight." It didn't mean anything at the time, but now... maybe that's it. Maybe that was why they all laughed and James cried. Maybe Daddy lost his Santa job and everyone knew it but me. He'd no longer fly his sleigh and deliver toys. The more I thought about it, the sadder I felt.

I shoved my hands between my legs and looked out the window.

I wandered through the flowery gardens outside a stuffy room that smelled like a hundred grandmas. Butterflies fluttered and I chased them.

In the middle of my chase, I remembered an early morning a few days ago when I last saw Daddy.

I woke in darkness to the sound of clanking dishes. I scurried barefoot to the kitchen to see Daddy making pancakes. I rounded the table and touched Daddy's fancy pilot's jacket that hung over the back of his chair. Daddy stood at the stove. He wore his white and dark blue work clothes, yellow stripes on his shoulder and shiny airplane pins on his collar. His belly pushed against his clothes and his shirt was barely tucked in. The grease from the sizzling cakes smelled sweet in the air and made my mouth fill with spit.

He pushed the spatula around and looked up. "Hey, little man. You're up early."

The tiled floor felt chilly, and my undersized pajamas were little warmth. I dove to him and wrapped my arms around his leg. He felt warm and smelled like Old Spice.

He messed my hair and continued cooking.

At the table, I sat on his lap and we ate from the same plate, something Mommy never let me do. The quiet of the morning made the house feel different, and having him to lean on felt safe.

"Daddy?" I asked with a mouthful.

"Yeah?"

"Why are pancakes heavier with syrup?" I pressed the top of one and some of the goo oozed up my fork.

"Syrup weighs it down." He poked a square piece with his fork and raised it to my mouth. "But that's what makes it good."

I sucked the square into my mouth like a vacuum, chewed, and swallowed. I licked the stickiness from my lips, and the maple sweetness returned.

After eating, we rinsed the plates in the sink and left the rest of the mess for Mommy. Daddy picked me up by the back of my pajama bottoms and flew me across the living room. I laughed out loud. He hushed me with a finger to his smiling lips. I covered my mouth with both hands but couldn't stop, and despite the wedgie, I peed a little.

He flew me into my bedroom, whispering, "Tower, do we have clearance for landing on runaway 327? Roger that." He landed me face-first into bed.

At the opposite side of the dark room, James lay in his bed. He slept like the dead, so I wasn't worried he'd wake.

I flopped to my back and hugged Daddy around the neck.

He poked a finger into my side.

I giggled and let go.

He moved toward the door.

"Daddy?"

"Yeah?" He neared.

"I love you."

He tapped the side of his nose. "See you in a few."

In the garden, I lay on the grass surrounded by flowers and stared at the puffy clouds above. Daddy's words echoed in my mind.

James's voice cut through my thoughts. "Mom's been looking all over for you."

I blinked and sat up. James towered over me.

I put my hand over my forehead to block the

sun. "Uh, I was–"

"You know, that was really stupid what you said in church."

I didn't know what to say. I kept squinting and looking up at him.

His tie looked crooked and the side of his shirt was untucked. He said, "You made some people cry."

I remembered seeing people cry, but I figured it was because they were laughing too hard. "Did I make you cry?"

He thumbed toward the building. "Get your butt back inside."

"You're not the boss of me."

He kicked me in my shoulder, and I toppled over. I grabbed my arm. "Ouch."

"Get inside."

"No!"

I jumped to my feet and ran.

"Christopher!"

I heard James' stomping shoes and felt the swipe of his hand on my back. I zigzagged through the bushes and flowers.

James called out bad words we weren't allowed to say. Then he said, "Jenny!"

I zipped behind a tree and stopped. Breathing hard. James came at me from one side, Jenny from the other.

I ran.

James dove and caught my legs.

I tumbled to the ground and rolled to my back. My eyes looked to the sky. A terrible thought hit me and the clouds looked spikey through my tears.

I sat up.

Jenny stood over me, angry, with her hands on her hips.

With James' red face, he looked ready to kill me. "You're such a little dork."

I spoke with a trembling voice, "I want Daddy."

Jenny said, "Daddy's gone."

I shook my head. "No. No he's not."

James said, "Yes. He's gone."

Jenny added, "We can't change it."

"He's not gone." I tried to stand, but I slipped on the dirt and fell hard on my butt.

James mumbled something to Jenny.

She said, "He's only five. He doesn't understand."

I yelled. "I do understand!" Tears hit me, filling up my nose and eyes. "I know but no one believes me." I wiped my face, and the two looked at me with waiting faces. I breathed tears and wiped again. "Daddy was Santa."

They didn't say anything.

I curled my legs into my chest and hugged them. "He was Santa." I wept.

Jenny nose was packed with snot.

James cried too, but didn't move. His eyes grew sparkly, and tears dripped down his cheeks. After a long silence, he said, "Yeah. You're right." He breathed and sounded like a little boy. "Daddy was Santa."

I hopped up and fell into him. He wrapped his arms around me. His body shook.

We stayed there for a long minute.

My mouth felt sticky and heavy like pancakes soaked in syrup. I remembered the early morning breakfast I spent with Daddy and I asked, "James?"

"What?"

"Why'd he have to be Santa?" I shivered.

He shook his head. "I don't know."

Jenny wrapped her arms around both of us and patted our backs. "C'mon. They're looking for us."

We made the long walk through the gardens. I thought about the Santa costume still lying on my bedroom floor at home. Though it felt forever away, I knew someday I'd fit into that red suit, and I'd be Santa – like Daddy. As much as it scared me, I hoped that day would hurry.

Story 2
The Drive

I feared this drive. Shivering, the cold Sunday morning after Christmas made my teeth chatter. The minivan's wheels crunched over salted streets. I passed houses weighed down in slushy white.

My wife and kids were still asleep, warm in their beds. I breathed and raked a hand through my thinning, graying hair. Marriage. Kids. Mortgage. Bills. How'd I get this old?

I turned onto the onramp. The highway lines blurred and my mind cleared, leaving nothing else to think about but him.

Granddad.

The stench of his stale cigars and smiling yellowed teeth were carved into my memory. It had been seven years. No, nine. After my third kid was born, making the trip was impossible. That's what I told myself. Our weekly calls turned into monthly calls, then every once in a while calls, and then never. The less we talked, the less we had to talk about. I actually blamed him for wasting my precious time. When we did talk, I knew he heard irritation in my voice. Even as a child, he had a knack of sensing my silent barometer, slipping me candies when Mom forced veggies on me and a wordless hand on the shoulder when tears welled up.

But now… he was gone.

Dad's phone call while I was in the middle of cycling the kids through their nightly routine left me breathless. I hung up and stared at my wife like someone had just murdered my childhood. I've been in a daze ever since, packing, rescheduling, staring.

An hour passed and the dark morning lightened,

but the freezing remained and made me want to pee. I pulled the car to the side of the road, jumped out, and ran to nearby bushes. Finished, I moseyed out and was half way back when I realized the minivan was gone. In its place was a blue and white car.

I stared. The highway was desolate in both directions. I spun from the bushes to the car.

A cold wind blew and I stuck my hands into my jacket pockets.

Clink.

My keys, but they felt different. I pulled them out. They looked strange yet familiar. I ran my finger over a Dodge insignia. I looked at the blue and white car and gasped.

"It's my…"

I stepped up to the car. It stood empty and quiet as if waiting for someone. I swept a hand over its slick roof. A pair of white racing stripes ran along the top. The sexy curved profile looked great even now. I hadn't thought about my Dodge Viper for years.

I opened the door, slipped inside, and breathed in the aroma of leather. From the rearview mirror hung a college graduation tassel, class of '92. I touched the dangling strands.

I gripped the key, stuck it in the ignition, and turned. The engine roared.

Overwhelmed, I laughed.

I ran a hand through my hair. "What the…?" I looked in the mirror. My head was covered with dark, wavy hair. My eyes looked bright and alert. I pulled at my face.

Car still rumbling, I looked down the highway. I had no idea what had happened, or what was happening. Still, I needed to get to Granddad's funeral.

I closed the door and shifted into gear. The engine's throttle was just like I remembered. The vibrations, the press against the seat, the immeasurable chills.

My parents thought I was crazy buying a brand new Viper right out of college. I had no job, student loans over my head, and no way of paying for anything. But Granddad believed. He gave me a pirate smile and punch to the shoulder from the passenger seat. The glint in his eyes negated the entire sensibility speech had Dad hammered me with. I didn't even mind Granddad lighting up a cigar in my new car. He believed in me. That was all I wanted.

So lost in my euphoric memories, I almost ran over a transient sleeping in my lane. I jerked the wheel. The car spun. I struggled.

The car jolted to a stop.

I breathed. A giant semi blared its horn at me. I was cockeyed in his lane. I hit the gas and wrenched the wheel until I was fully in the median.

The truck flew past. A gust of wind rocked the car.

I unbuckled and stepped outside. The bum still lay sleeping in the lane. I crossed the icy road and ran to him.

I knelt. "Hey, buddy." I touched. The pile of clothes shifted revealing a trash bag, no man.

Disgruntled, I jogged back up the road.

I stopped. Dodge Viper was gone. Instead, there stood a cream-orange AMC Gremlin hatchback, my first car. I crossed the highway and circled it. Empty and idling, its keys hung in the ignition. I opened the creaking door and sat. Even in the cold, I smelled the B.O. The engine clunked, struggling to maintain idle. I grabbed the wheel remembering how much I loved this piece of junk.

I shifted into gear and drove off. A car honked and swerved around me. The wheel shook nervously.

I moved my leg and knocked the rabbit foot keychain dangling from the ignition. I grabbed it.

Granddad handed me the keys on my fifteenth birthday, rabbit foot and all.

Dad snatched them away from me.

"Oh, come on." Granddad's stubbled face bent into a smile. "Who's going to be my designated driver?"

Dad's eyes burned at him. "Wouldn't be a problem if you'd lay off the booze."

That night, Granddad snuck to my room, threw a jacket over me, and whispered, "C'mon, boy."

We snuck out and I drove this crappy Gremlin through darkened city streets, Granddad laughing next to me, beer in one hand, cigar in the other.

Now, heading down the highway, I felt the weight of no longer having such a powerful man in my life. He was a horrible influence and I loved him for it. Unlike my peers, he'd get away with everything, filling me with a whirlwind of childlike adventure.

I looked at my body. It was thin, scrawny. I was a teenager.

I turned off an exit, maneuvering through familiar

streets I hadn't seen in years. Same trees, same houses, same unpaved roads.

My heart leapt. The sadness of losing Granddad had somehow evaporated. I felt excited, happy.

I whipped around a tight curve, closed my eyes, and shouted, "Yahoo!"

I felt cold wind over my face.

Opening my eyes, I was no longer driving. I rode my blue bicycle. Granddad had painted my name on its side. Legs pumped the pedals. I was a kid.

I laughed, sped down Granddad's steep driveway, and slammed on the brakes.

His small, red house stood in front of me, the wooden porch he built himself looked fresh.

The front door opened.

I ran and jumped up the steps.

Granddad stepped out. "Hello, boy."

I hugged him, then looked up. "Tell me a story."

He gave me his pirate smile, cigar dangling, teeth yellow. "Ever tell you about the boy who time traveled?"

We walked in. I shivered inside, hungry for his story.

I knew it was going to be good.

Story 3
Living in Illusions

John's Shorts
short stories - volume 1

Living in Illusions

John Hope

Outside in the snow, Mike shivered, already weary from visiting his mom before it happened. He loved Mom, but over the past few years love wore heavily on him.

The house keys rattled in his fingers as snow battered his back like burning pins. He knew Mom was inside and he never liked forcing her to strain her frail body to the door.

Inside, he closed the door and in the foyer brushed off the powdery white from his coat. He peered into the living room.

Sitting next to a dim fire, his mom smiled from her rocker. She lowered the paperback in her hands, her eyes watery. "Michael."

"Hi, Mom." Mike struggled to keep his balance as he wiggled out of his wet galoshes.

Mom pulled the handmade blanket onto her lap. She rocked in slow motion. The chair squeaked.

Mike dropped his coat in the hall and shuffled to the fire. "I haven't seen it this bad since Dad took us out to pick up a Christmas tree that one year. Remember? We drove out to Old Man Silverton's farm and ... are you okay, Mom?"

"Yes. I'm fine." Her words sounded sad and weak. She wiped her teary eyes. "I'm just a little run down. That's all."

Mike picked up a split log next to the fire and tossed it in. He nudged it with the poker. "You still hauling in all this firewood by yourself? I told you to call up Pete Collins whenever–"

"I know, I know. It's not that. Actually, I was just thinking about your father."

"Oh."

"I can't help it around Christmas. He loved the whole thing. Decorating, shopping, watching you kids open up gifts. Oh, he was a little kid himself." She smiled, her eyes drifted to the fire, snapping around the new log.

"Yeah." Mike lowered to the couch, the sweet smell of burning pine bringing back memories of his childhood. He rubbed his face. His hands felt cool and rough. "I remember when he used to throw me on his shoulders and make me hang those lights up on that overhang." He chuckled. "Felt like he was going to tip over and crack my head open on the pavement."

"He always meant well. He always looked out for you kids."

"I know."

"He was a good man." She sighed. "A good man."

Mike's mind swirled with warm images, feelings, memories he'd kept at arm's length. He looked to Mom, who continued rocking with a distant look. "You know," he thought how to phrase the statement, "there's one Christmas I really didn't understand."

"Understand what?" She straightened, her glassy

eyes drifting toward Mike.

"Do you remember Bobby Hillsfield? He played for the Blue Jays and was an amazing home run hitter."

"Oh, yes. You wouldn't stop talking about him."

"Well, there was this one season he broke Hank Aaron's career homerun record and I just had to have that jersey with his number and Home Run King on the back. And I was so excited I kept on asking you two about it before Christmas. You wouldn't budge, but one day Dad pulled me aside when you weren't looking and said he just picked it up for me."

She smirked. "That rascal."

"Then Christmas morning came, but no jersey. I asked Dad about it but he just shrugged and said, 'Oh well.'"

Mom shook her head with thoughtful intent. "I don't remember that."

"He lied to me. Why did he do that?"

She breathed deep. "I'm sure he had his reasons."

Mike stared at her, waiting for a better answer. Nothing.

A few minutes passed, Mike gazing into to dancing flames while he pondered.

Mom coughed. "Think I'm going to head to bed early." She struggled out of the rocker. "I've got that doctor's appointment in the morning." She dropped the blanket into the chair. "Don't stay up too late." Mike nodded. "Goodnight, Mom."

A couple hours later, the quick clanging of dishes snapped Mike from his book. He frowned, wondering why Mom was awake. She never woke this late in the evening.

Mike jumped up and shot to the kitchen. He froze at the sight of a large man in a white fluffy dress, rummaging through cabinets.

"Uh…" Mike tried to speak.

"Don't you guys have any Pop-Tarts?" The man spoke, adjusting the tiara on his wind-swept hair. "It's practically un-American not to have Pop-Tarts."

Mike's mind exploded with a volley of questions, none of which could encapsulate the ludicrousness standing before him.

The man turned to Mike, hands on his hips, a fairy-like wand gripped in one fist. He was clean-shaven, but chest hair spouted from his dress. "Oh, how impolite of me." He held out a hand. "My name's Nelson and I'm the Christmas Angel who's supposed to grant you a wish since you saved that lady from the fire."

Mike didn't shake his hand. "Uh… fire?" The words felt stuck in his throat.

"Ooo." Nelson maneuvered around Mike toward an open-door pantry. "So you do have Pop-Tarts. Don't mind if I do." He ripped open a package. "You know, fire. That really hot stuff that human flesh doesn't like."

"What fire… er… what lady?"

"Please, please. Don't be bashful." The angel jammed two entire Pop-Tarts into his wide mouth at once. "Um. Hea-ben."

"I haven't the slightest…" Thoughts fluttered through this mind like dizzying moths. "…wait. You're an angel?"

The angel swallowed his mouthful in one gulp. "Come. Come. At least be a little grateful. Heck you're the best stop I've got tonight. After you I got a couple kids who walked an old man across the street. Big whoop. At least you made the newspapers." He ripped open the next pair of Pop-

Tarts with his teeth and jammed them into his mouth.

"Wait a minute." He snapped his fingers. "I think I know what you're talking about." Mike stepped back, grabbing a counter for support, as if subconsciously trying to anchor himself in this bizarre conversation. "I remember reading about a Mike Ziffabihger who saved some girl in an office fire."

"Um…" The angel swallowed. "And?"

"I'm a different Mike Ziffabihger."

"What? You mean you're not the same Mike Ziffabihger? How many Mike Ziffabihgers are there in this town? Is he your cousin or something?"

"No." He gave him a crooked smile. "No relation."

The angel smacked his forehead. "Man. I hate it when this happens." He waved the empty box in his hand and looked disappointed. "I guess I'll be on my way." He tossed the empty box into the pantry. "See ya."

Mike backed up a step as the angel's opaque image lightened to a translucency. He blurred and sparkles swirled around him. The swirling stopped, and he suddenly returned to focus.

"You know," the angel began. "What the heck. I'm already here and I ate your Pop-Tarts. I might as well grant you a Christmas wish too."

"Ah… okay." Mike gave a clumsy nod.

"So, what do you want?"

"Ah… well, what is a Christmas wish?" Mike grabbed the back of his neck.

"It's like any ol' wish except this just comes from a Christmas Angel. Please don't make me get into all the details. It'll bore you to pieces. Besides, I believe I was asleep that day in Christmas Angel School." He stepped to the kitchen table, sat in a chair, and propped his feet up on the counter.

Mike cringed at the less than heavenly details he'd rather the angel kept hidden below his dress.

Nelson continued, "I'll make it easy for you. You tell me what you want. It can be anything. Anything you can think of. And it will be yours. My most popular choices are money and power and fame. But I gotta warn you, those aren't usually the best choices."

"I can imagine." Mike eased to the side and shot a quick look out into the hallway, hoping Mom was still asleep. "Um … I don't know."

"If you need some time I could swing by the

other Mike Ziffabihger's and get his order then swing back your way."

"Well, okay."

"You got it, buddy." Nelson hopped to his feet. "See ya."

"Actually," Mike said.

Nelson raised his eyebrows. "You know what you want?"

"Yeah."

"Good, it'll save me a trip. What'll it be?"

Mike shot another glance toward the hallway. "I want my father back."

"Okay, let me just look up where he is." He spun around inside a translucent, sparkling cloud for a couple seconds. He returned. "Ick. Are you kidding me? He's been dead for five years. What do you plan to do with him?" He stepped back. "Hey, you're not one of those sickos who plays around with corpses, are you?"

"No, I meant I want him back alive."

"Oh. Ha, ha. Silly me. I knew that, really. I was just … ah…" He coughed, then rubbed his hands together. "One live father it is." He hesitated. "Are you sure? You only get the one wish."

Mike breathed deep. "Yes. Yes, I'm sure. My

mom is so lonely without him. Please. Bring my dad back."

"Okay. One father coming up. It's been nice knowing you."

He again spun into a sparkling cloud. Seconds later a silent flash of light forced Mike to look away. When he reopened his eyes, Nelson was gone, the kitchen dark and silent.

A hollow thunk at the door drew Mike away. A series of random turns of the doorknob followed.

Mike rushed to the front door and opened it.

"Dad!" Mike fell into his father's arms. The stench of stale liquor smacked Mike in the face.

"What the hell is your problem?" the old man slurred. He shoved his son away and staggered inside. "What's for dinner? I'm starving." His left hand grabbed hold of anything he passed while his right clenched a bottle wrapped in a brown paper bag.

Mike rushed to his father's side. "Let me get your coat."

His dad raised his arms. "Get your hands off of me. It's too damn cold in here without a coat." He stumbled into the living room. "You call that a fire? I've told that woman time and time again not to waste those logs with a sorry fire like that." He plopped down on the couch. "Where is she, anyhow? Martha!"

"Shhhh." Mike scurried to the side of the couch. "Dad, Mom's sleeping."

"What? At this hour? Something's wrong with her. She's just damned lazy. Always was. You got something cookin'?"

Mike pulled the rocker toward the couch and sat. "You'll be fine in the morning. It's just the liquor talking."

"Liquor my ass. It's your mother. That hag's a worthless bag of skin. You've got to teach them. Remember that, son, when you find a woman." He shook the bagged bottle at Mike's face. "Believe me, I've tried to teach your mother. Hell, just last week, I was teaching her good when she faked that coma to get herself out of work. Is she still faking it? That where she is?"

The truth in the drunk man's words hit Mike like a punch to the face. His mother slipped into a coma a week before his dad impaled himself after slamming his car into a tree. The memories flooded back to Mike. He'd never made the connection between his dad and the coma. When she woke a week later, she had partial memory loss and could not recall any of the beatings. Nor could she justify the bruises.

Mike and his siblings ultimately slipped into the same illusionary world. They forgot the abuse. They forgot the screaming, the fights, and the alcoholism.

They forgot the pain.

Mike stood, turned away, and rubbed his face. He wondered why he'd been so foolish to forget what a bastard the man had been. After his dad died, every recollection was something positive, something good.

That is, except one.

"Dad, I have a question for you. Remember a long time ago when I wanted that Bobby Hillsfield's jersey and you said that you got it for me but…"

"Oh, yeah. That shmuck. You know I met that guy down at Maken's Bar? He made a proposition to me."

"Proposition?"

"Yeah." He winked. "Guy on guy. Something with a big group. Gross stuff."

Mike looked at his dad.

He continued, "Said he'd make me a good deal. He wanted money. I wasn't going to let any kid of mine get messed up with all that." He leaned his head back and took another swig from the bottle. "And another thing…" He leaned forward and collapsed to the floor. His body rose and fell with every grinding snore.

Mike stood there, staring at his father's back.

The man snored.

Mike slunk backwards and sat down in the rocker, gazing into the dying fire, quiet, his mind racing.

His image of Bobby Hillsfield crumbled. Up to this point, he still looked up to the man, admired him, and even occasionally fantasized being him. After all the dreams and all the envious thoughts, all he could think of now was Bobby Hillsfield sniffing and injecting with dozens of other fellow druggies.

Mike stared at his pitiful father. His mother was right. Even though he did beat her and even though he was an alcoholic, this pathetic man did always look out for him and his sisters.

A familiar voice stopped his thoughts like a slap to the back. "Man, this was your wish?"

Mike snapped his head up.

Nelson stood behind the couch.

Mike said, "Hey, uh, Nelson. Lost again?"

"No, smartass, I'm not lost again. The other Mike apparently moved out to North Dakota last week. Out of my district. But apparently you get another wish."

"Another wish?"

"Ah, man." Nelson shook his head. "We don't have to go through this again, do we?"

"No." Mike stood. "But why another?"

"Since you used the last wish for your mother just to make her happy, that qualifies for a bonus wish." He winked.

"Bonus wish?"

"Yeah. Woulda told you earlier, but bonus wishes require additional paperwork and…"

"But…" Mike propped his hands on his hips. "What about the other wish you gave me? Wasn't that a bonus wish?"

"Okay, you got me." Nelson threw his hands up. "The first one was a freebee and I forgot about the bonus. In any case, tonight's your lucky night. So what'll it be?" He stepped closer to Mike. "You don't have any dead brothers you want me to call out of the grave, do you?"

"No, actually, I…" He looked at his father and paused a second. "Actually, I want you to take him back."

"What? Take him back?" He stepped around the couch, studying the passed out man. "But you just got him."

"I know. I… please, just take him back."

"Are you sure? Man, you really have to bone up on your wishing skills. This is two for two. You're missing out on some really cool stuff."

"Yes, I'm sure. Please, take him back."

"Okay." He slapped and rubbed his hands together. "Hopefully, I won't be back again tonight. See ya."

The whirlpool formed. In a flash both Nelson and Mike's father were gone.

Mike stood quietly in the dimming room for several seconds, the crackling of the fire puffing out tiny streams of smoke and piney scents. In the quiet room, Mike felt an empty void like being a survivor of a deadly storm.

He walked upstairs to his mom's room and leaned against the bedroom doorframe for a long time, watching her sleep. He breathed, feeling the warmth of home and knowing all was right in the world, or at least right then, right there.

He headed out to his car, retrieved his suitcase, and made his way to the guest bedroom where he'd sleep that night, and probably the next few.

Lying down on the stiff sheets, he made a mental note for the morning: Buy more Pop-Tarts.

Story 4
Recalculating

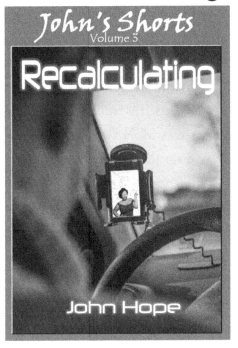

I closed the car door, gripped the steering wheel, and prepared for death. Midnight. My car rested in the quiet, St. Pete neighborhood outside the crappy, two bed, one bath house that I no longer owned. A prowling cat stepped across the empty, narrow street a few houses down, a harsh streetlight lighting her way. Kept a secret, I knew that neither the cat nor any of my formal numbskull neighbors knew what I had planned—a plunge into Tampa Bay.

With the turn of the key, the engine struggled and coughed. "C'mon, c'mon," It caught and rumbled to life.

I caught myself peering through the rearview mirror for oncoming traffic though I know everyone's asleep in this suburban nook. The only life at this hour was miles away in the clubs and bars downtown. Even if there was another car, the boxes, lampshades, and stacks of laundry stacked in the backseat blocked my view.

I pulled from the curb and glanced back at the darkened house one last time. Foreclosure was the last in a long line of dominos that have crashed down on me over the past year. *Had it only been three years?* Three years ago, I was married to my love, Diana, owned a house together, was employed and living the high life. I had hobbies—fishing and model airplanes. I had life. I had hope. Now, look at me. A shell of a man, bankrupted, widowed, homeless…alone.

I combed my hand through my thinning hair and coasted through a couple of stop signs out to 66th Street. The green traffic light blasted at my face, but

I didn't move. There was nobody honking at me to get my butt moving.

Despite my delay, my mind was made up. Death was the only answer. However, I sucked at directions. I'd moved to St. Pete five years ago, yet I still didn't know my way around. I dug into my pocket and pulled out my cell phone. Opening Google Maps, I typed in Skyway Bridge. Images swirled, quietly thinking, and then went black. I tapped at the screen, but nothing. "Dang it..." Perfect timing for my phone to go dead.

Now what?

I twisted to the clutter in the backseat, as if hoping it possessed the answer. Then a thought struck me: the old GPS.

I leaned, opened the glove box, and dug out my GPS. Straightening, I plugged the power cord into the car's cigarette lighter and waited as it booted up. Its welcoming chime felt comforting. I hadn't used it for years. The last couple of years had been spent shuttling to and from the hospital with Diana, watching her grow shriveled and weak. I knew the turns to the hospital blindfolded. Now, when heading for the final drive of my life, I hadn't a clue where to go.

"Welcome, Alister," the GPS spoke to me. "Where might I take you today?"

We had to go with the fully voice-activated GPS; Diana insisted. She paid extra for the deluxe GPS software, intending to amend my horrible lack of direction. She even went out of her way to download and install Tyesha, a non-standard voice that Diana said reminded her of her college roommate. And she programmed in details like my name and common destinations.

"Hello, Tyesha," I said. "To the Skyway Bridge."

"You got it, Alister. Sunshine Skyway Bridge. Calculating route." More chimes. "Okay. Turn right onto 66th Street North."

I breathed, gripped the wheel tighter, and made the turn.

Chills tickled through my body. *I'm doing this.* The end. No more anxiety pills. No more all-night drunken stupors trying to forget the pain. No more unpaid bills, and calls from collection offices, and wailing into my pillow, punching the walls, and wondering why I existed. For once in a long, long time, I felt an enormous weight lifted off my chest. I was finally doing something with my life—ending it.

Tyesha's voice spoke, "Please specify your

ultimate destination."

"Uh?" I thought, *ultimate destination*? Of course, I knew this answer. But why was the GPS asking me? "Um… the Skyway Bridge."

"Yes, understood," she said. "But the Sunshine Skyway Bridge is not a valid destination. It's a bridge. Where will the bridge lead you?"

I shook my head. This GPS was a bit too smart for its own good. "Just take me to the Skyway Bridge." I pause, then said under my breath. "Stop giving me trouble."

"Trouble? Boy, I'm trying to help you out. I ain't givin' you no trouble."

I slowed the car and pulled over to the side of the road, staring at the glowing GPS. "You didn't just say that."

"You better believe I did. Now, whatcha got planned for the Skyway Bridge? That sucka be the scariest bridge ever."

"This is too weird." I yanked out the power cord and the device's screen blacked out. I rubbed my eyes, trying to readjust to the sudden darkness. Picking up the powerless GPS, I spun it in my hands. "Where the heck did you get this thing, Diana?"

The GPS lit up. "Oh, no you didn't!"

I jerked. The GPS hit the passenger-side floorboard.

Tyesha's voice continued. "Whatcha doin' yankin' my power cord? I don't think so."

"Wha-wha?"

"Yo, butter fingers. C'mon. Pick me up from this nasty ol' floor. Dang. Ain't you never heard of a vacuum?"

Despite my better judgement, I leaned to the floor and retrieved the GPS. I squinted at its glow. The map displayed with the next turn 2.5 miles away. Below the map, Tyesha's last comments were spelled out in bold text.

A cursor bounced as she continued to speak. "So, like I was asking before you dun yanked out my power cord, where you think you goin'? Don't tell me you wanna take your butt to middle of the Skyway so you can do a little swan dive into the Gulf."

"Well, the thing is…"

"Oh, snap. That was what you were thinkin'! Ah, no. I ain't havin' no part of that. I start assisting suicides and the next thing you know I'm a voice box in some creepy Betsey Wetsy that'll sit on a shelf and scare a little girl enough to make her wet the bed. Not me. Not today."

I stuttered, "Wha-wha are…Why…H-h-how are you even working?"

"Don't you worry your little head about that. Diana dun fixed me up, just right. She knew you got no sense of direction. That was obvious on your first date with Diana when you got her address wrong and knocked on the door on the house across the street. Diana had to run to the rescue and peel off that weird cross-dressing man who wrapped his arms around your leg, begging you to take him out to dinner."

"How'd you know…?"

"Boy, I know lots of things. This electronic brain of mine ain't just full of maps."

"Obviously," I muttered.

"Do I detect a bit of sass? Now that's more like yourself. Heck, it wasn't long ago when you were on the ball, speaking up like nobody's business."

"Wha-" I spun my head back and forth, convinced somebody must be putting me on. There were enough punked vines on social networks to believe someone must have been controlling the GPS remotely. A pair of cars passed on the six-lane street. Otherwise, the road was desolate, with a closed McDonald's and Jiffy Lube on one side and a darkened apartment complex on the other. A mosquito tapped past the windshield, the overhead streetlight probably attracting it to my car.

"Don't you remember?" Tyesha asked.

I blinked, refocusing on the glowing device in my hand. "Remember what?"

"Dang, boy. What you need is a trip down memory lane. Recalculating route."

"Route? What route?"

Her voice took a more professional tone. "In one mile, turn right onto 38th Avenue North."

I stared.

The device glowed. A cursor blinked at the end of Tyesha's last sentence.

She harped, "Well? You gonna get movin' or what?"

I took a deep breath. Obviously, this quirky gismo that Diana set up wasn't going to guide me to the bridge anytime soon. I guessed a little detour wouldn't hurt, as long as she eventually led me to the bridge.

I checked the rearview mirror and pulled away from the curb, the night's city lights speeding past as

I accelerated.

Tyesha said, "Turn right at the next light."

I complied.

Tyesha continued her instructions, leading me down one vacant street and the next until she ordered, "Stop in front of Azalea Park."

The brakes squeaked to a stop and I shifted into *park*. With the engine quietly idling, I looked left and right, half-expecting something to jump out at me. Instead, an open, unlit city park sat peacefully to my left while a row of small houses lined the opposite side of the street, their porchlights casting shadows. "Well, Tyesha? Now what?"

"We're here."

"Where's here?"

"Don't you remember nothin'? Angle that melon of yours to the left. Don't you remember that concert a few years back?"

"Oh. You mean that Battle of the Bands thing? What about it?"

"Are your circuits fried? Don't you remember the crowds on the verge of a riot?"

I shrugged. "I was working security. That was my job."

"Your job? Alister, you dun' took your job to the

next level that day and saved the lives of hundreds, thousands."

I rolled my eyes. "I wouldn't go that far."

"You wouldn't? Well, let me refresh your memory of what exactly happened. This little ol' park outside your car was packed full with an unprecedented crowd that day. They estimated a hundred or two would attend. Instead, thousands and thousands showed up. Men, women, and children packed shoulder to shoulder, pressing for that stage. Some yelling and jumping to the music they could barely hear. Some getting sick from the sweat of compacted bodies and the day's humidity."

"It was hot that—"

"Chill! I'm tellin' the story. Now, where was I? Oh, yeah. The crowds. Then, the worst happened. A rain storm blew in and the power went out. Now, there were thousands trapped in the crowd, no music, rain, people getting sick and barfing like they just heard Donald Trump belt out *Amazing Grace*. Amid this disaster, who came to the rescue? Alister the security guard. You jumped up on that stage with a high-powered bull horn and got everyone's attention. You somehow got them all to play the biggest game of Simon Says, followed by singing a few verses of *One-Hundred Bottles of Beer on the Wall*."

I winced with embarrassment. "That's all I could think of at the time."

"That's just it. You didn't have to be a genius to save the day. You just needed to get everyone to focus and not flip out. That stupid little game and song were just what that crowd needed to save them from themselves. After several minutes, the rain subsided, the cops dispersed the crowds, and everyone went home. You didn't a win a medal. You weren't crowned king of corny entertainment. But you were the hero that day."

I rubbed my chin as I surveyed the darkened park. "That was just one day. One little blip in a very mediocre life."

"*Tsk*. You still don't get it, do you? C'mon. We headin' to example number two. Recalculating route. Travel five hundred feet to 13th Avenue North and turn left."

I shook my head, shifted into drive, and followed Tyesha's instructions.

Before we even reached it, I knew Tyesha was leading me to the St. Pete General Hospital—a place I'd spent months agonizing over Diana's fate. I turned off early into a vacant church parking lot near the hospital and shifted into *park*.

"Yo, Magellan," Tyesha quipped. "You turned off too soon."

I shook my head. "I'm not going there."

"I'm only guiding you there—"

"I know why," I snapped. "I've wasted way too many hours of life there already. I'm never going back."

"Wasted? You think your time with Diana was a waste?"

"No. It's not that."

"Then what the heck do you mean?"

I struggled for the words. "She...she died anyhow! She died...despite everything they did to her." Tears poured. "If I'd known how it was all going to end, I would've rather spent our time at home, or better yet on a beach in Hawaii."

"You hate the beach."

"I know that!" I wiped my sniffling nose. "But Diana loved it."

"So what you're sayin' is you'd go somewhere just to make Diana happy."

"Of course."

"Well, wouldn't you know it? That's exactly what you did."

"Huh?"

"Didn't you ever realize that Diana wanted to be at the hospital? She wanted to be there because she wouldn't ever give up. She was going to fight that cancer to the inch of her life. In fact, that's exactly what she did. And you, Mr. *I-Hate-The-Beach*, were the one who made that happen for her. You took her there. You sat next to her throughout each chemo treatment. You supported her when she needed it. You gave her the strength to fight the battle that she wanted to fight."

A lull followed as Tyesha's words sunk in. I stared at the brightly-lit hospital parking lot just beyond a line of blunt hedges that separated it from the church. As much as I loved Diana and took care of her, I hadn't seen her illness from her perspective. Not really. Tyesha was right. Diana wanted to fight. And yes, she never gave up on anything—even on the littlest things.

I recalled a time when we went through a Burger King drive-thru and were given fries instead of the onion rings we ordered. I told her that I was okay with the fries, but Diana wouldn't have it. She forced me to park and marched into the restaurant.

Then, things escalated when the lady behind the

register refused to swap it out since we weren't actually up-charged for the onion rings. I tried to interject, offering to pay for a new order of onion rings. But again, Diana wouldn't have it. The thing was, she didn't just complain. She explained at length to the lady behind the counter about the importance of customer service and how this skill would carry her into any future jobs where she may have to swallow her pride and do the right thing for the sake of the situation. In that moment, I saw a tenacity in Diana that I hadn't noticed before. She wasn't so much concerned about the onion rings. Rather, she wanted to do the right thing and only the right thing.

I saw the same tenacity in those final months of her life. To her, her illness was the enemy. And she sacrificed her life, taking on multiple rounds of treatment to rid herself of what was wrong. Tyesha was right. Diana wanted to be there, and no one would ever stop her.

"The problem is…" I muttered at last. "…Diana is gone. Even if I did help her, with her gone, why do I need to be here anymore? And I don't just mean, at the hospital."

"My, my, Alister. You need another example,

don't cha?"

"No. No more examples. Take me to the Skyway Bridge. I command you."

"Oh, you command me. Look at me. I'm shakin' in my diodes."

I picked up the GPS from the center console. "I could chuck you out the window right now."

"Uh, c'mon. Be reasonable."

I lifted my hand, ready to throw. "Reasonable?"

"Okay, okay. Take a chill pill. I'll take to you the bridge."

I lowered my hand.

"Recalculating route. Turn right onto 38th Avenue."

I followed Tyesha's instructions.

For several minutes, I drove in near-silence. Tyesha occasionally pierced the quiet with her flatly-spoken directions.

We eventually merged onto the fast-moving I-275. Lights sped past the opposite side of the highway and the persistent rumble of tires on asphalt provided a strange sense of comfort. The mile markers ticked past like the remaining minutes of my life.

Signs for the Skyway Bridge and the nearing toll

plaza quickened my heart. I drove through a SunPass-Only lane through the plaza, though I didn't have a transponder. *Go ahead, send me a ticket.* I smiled, feeling more and more confident that I'd made the right choice to end it here and now.

We traversed a causeway that led to the main spans of the bridge. I wiggled my sweaty palms over the steering wheel but kept my focus. *I'm doing this. I'm really doing this.*

"You know, there's still time," Tyesha said. "You don't have to go through with this."

I tightened my lips. "It's too late. Much too late."

The car started its 400-foot climb up to the bridge's apex that provided clearance to shipping in and out of Tampa Bay. Winds rocked the car, forcing me to grip the wheel tighter. I envisioned my leap into the black water below. My veins pulsated on the sides of my head.

"So, just out of curiosity," Tyesha started, "are you planning on plunging your car off into the water?"

"No. I'll pull over." I paused. "You'll be safe and dry, Tyesha."

"Good. I've got plenty of other people to help out."

"Don't you mean hassle?"

"There goes that sass again." Her cursor blinked. "I sure wish you'd reconsider. I mean, I've grown to like that snarky voice of yours."

"I'm sorry, too." I reached the summit and eased the car to the side. I shut off the engine. The car went dark, although bright greenish-yellow lights from the bridge pierced the car windows. Their brightness made Tampa Bay below appear invisibly black.

Tyesha said, "For the record, I'm gonna miss you."

"Yeah…I'll miss you, too." I paused. "Goodbye, Tyesha."

I stepped out of the car, rounded the front to the rails lining the bridge's side. The deep emptiness looking out to the Gulf combined with the wind's turbulence gave me the impression of standing on the edge of giant vacuum. I peered over the side of the railing toward the water. Directly below me, purple floodlights lit the bridge's pylons and the choppy water, which caused the tips of the water's chop to sparkle.

Headlights of an approaching car from behind made me squint. I waited for it to pass. As it did, however, the brakes squeaked. The car pulled to the side of the road ahead of me.

I gripped the railing. "Just what I need," I muttered to myself. "A damned Good Samaritan."

The car's driver exited. But instead of him coming to me, his shadowy silhouette rounded his vehicle and approached the railing near his car.

I stood, waiting for his approach. It never came. In fact, he stood at the railing, as if preparing to jump himself.

"Are you kidding me?" I whispered.

I looked out to the water. The vacuum that urged me forward a moment ago seemed to have lost its strength. I still felt it's pull, but my concern for the other person fifty yards away stifled its affect. My fingers slipped on the railing's cool metal. I bit the side of my lip and peered toward the other man.

Taking a deep breath, I stepped toward him.

As I neared, I noticed he was sitting on the railing, his legs dangling out toward the water. A mere rock forward of his head and he'd tumble off the bridge.

A car passed us when I was within ten yards of the man. He turned toward me. His eyes widened.

I gasped. "Kyle?"

"Alister?" he replied. "I didn't see you..." He gripped the rail.

I didn't have to ask why Kyle was here. He and I befriended each other at the stress counseling center that my therapist recommended to me. He wasn't married, living with and caring for his mother who was grappling with dementia. In Diana's final days, I stopped going to the center. When I used to go, I had long talks with Kyle in the nearby 24-hour Coffee Hut following our meetings. Those talks were far more heeling and stress-relieving then any of the nonsense that the center or my therapist threw at me. The irony was that Kyle was one of the most depressive people I knew. He'd go on and on about how he never left home and how he hated people calling him a momma's boy even though he knew it to be true. My constant barrage of encouragement toward him somehow made its way to my ears. When I stopped going to the center, I stopped meeting him, and I stopped hearing those *Don't Give Up* speeches that poured out of me.

"What's going on, Kyle?"

The bridge's lights glistened his teary eyes despite the persistent wind drying our faces. "Mother's dead."

I waited a beat before replying. "I'm sorry."

"Why'd you leave the center?"

"I…" I shook my head. "I guess I gave up."

He looked out to the dark water, his butt teetered on the narrow railing. "I thought at least you'd be at the Coffee Hut."

"Sorry."

"Yeah, well. I guess everybody's sorry." He looked to me. "How'd you know I'd be here?"

I peered back to my car. For a moment, I almost forgot why I was here. "I didn't know." I returned my focus to him. "But maybe I was supposed to be here."

He coughed and choked out tears. "No. Just dumb luck finding me here, I'm sure."

"Luck? Luck had nothing to do with me being here. Just like it wasn't lucky that we met at the center." As I said these words, memories and images overcame me. Me calling out *Simon Says* commands to the crowds of people at Azalea Park. Chatting with Kyle at the late-night Coffee Hut well into the wee hours of the morning. The long hours sitting next to Diana in the cold cancer infusion centers. None of these memories were the result of luck. Each experience was as necessary for me as it was for others. "I'm supposed to be here," I muttered, louder than I meant to.

"Supposed to?" Kyle asked.

"I've had so many experiences. They've kept me focused on others so I wouldn't have to think of myself. Like a GPS, telling me which way to turn my head. As I recall from our long talks, you're not much different, Kyle. Your mother kept you focused. And at the Coffee Hut, we kept each other on track." I gazed at the purple darkness beyond the railing. "You can't leave. I need you. We need each other."

Kyle grimaced. "Damn it, Alister." He sniffled. "No matter how horrible I want to feel, you say crap like that and it makes me feel better." He shook his head. "You are like Mother."

I smile. "And I look just a good in a dress."

He chuckled quietly. "Wise ass." He shifted to swing one leg over the railing toward me, but his heel hit, and he slipped.

I leapt forward and caught his arm.

He grabbed my shoulder with his other hand. "Holy shit," he gasped.

I leaned backward, sliding his body over the rail and onto the safety of the bridge. I landed on my back, Kyle lying on top of me.

I said, "I hope you never did *this* with your mother."

"Well, we were close." We both laughed.

He rolled off me and we struggled to our feet. My bones cracked on the way up.

We panted and gazed at each other for a long moment, a wordless *now what?* falling over both of us.

Blue flashing lights hit us as a police officer pulled up. Without getting out, he spoke through his opened, passenger-side window. "What's going on, fellas?"

Kyle had that *little-kid-caught-with-his-hand-in-the-cookie-jar* look.

I patted Kyle's shoulders with my arm and said, "It's okay, officer. We just got a little lost. We're leaving now."

He narrowed his eyes at us. "Can't have you stopping on the middle of the bridge."

Kyle said, "Yes. We're leaving."

"Okay. Hop in your cars." He kept idling next to us, blocking the outside lane.

I looked to Kyle. "Meet you at the Coffee Hut?"

Kyle hesitated. "I'm not sure how to get there

from here."

I smiled and nodded. "Follow me."

I got back into my car and right away Tyesha lit up. She said, "Welcome back! Or are you gonna throwing me into the Gulf after all?"

"Na," I said. "Not yet. Please take me to the Coffee Hut."

Tyesha's lights seemed to glitter with happiness. "All-righty then! Recalculating."

Story 5

Beyond the Closed Door

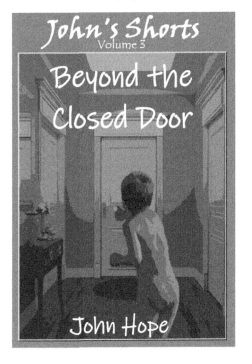

Trevor sprang awake to the clatter of jingle bells out in the hallway. He clenched Beary, his favorite stuffed animal, as a single thought filled his mind: *Santa Claus.*

His bare feet hit his bedroom floor. He dropped

Beary, snatched the Batman flashlight he kept on his dresser, and dashed for his door. Hinges creaked and a door handle clicked. Trevor hesitated, fearing Santa might have heard him.

Heavy footsteps on hardwood followed by a metal screech let Trevor know he was probably detected.

Biting the side of his lip, he considered returning to bed. But his curiosity wouldn't let him. Trevor pushed open his door and tiptoed down the hallway toward the living room.

He stopped and clicked on his flashlight. Mommy's baking flour and a half-dozen tiny jingle bells littered the floor between the unlit Christmas tree and the hallway. He'd set this trap for Santa, giving the eight-year-old concrete proof of the jolly man's existence. Trevor's squeaked at the sight of jingle bells' positions near the wall, kicked away from where he'd carefully placed them hours before.

He swung the beam of light up the hallway and noticed flour-laden footprints leading toward the closet that Trevor had been forbidden to enter at Christmastime. Excited, he scurried for the closet and reached for the handle.

He balked.

Thoughts of his fellow second graders' teasing laughter a couple weeks ago consumed his mind. They pointed at him and told everyone how stupid he was that he still believed in Santa. He ran home that day crying. He buried his head in his pillow and thought about the closet. As much as he didn't want to admit it, the other kids' painful, "There's no Santa," made sense. If Mommy and Daddy bought the presents, they would have hidden them in the closet. He crept to the closet that day while Mommy cooked dinner and awaited Daddy's arrival from work. He couldn't open it then. Behind that door marked the end of something within him— something fragile and precious. Opening the closet door and seeing the presents meant he could never believe in Santa again, never believe in his magic, and never be that excited little boy at Christmas.

Now, he felt the same fear. There could be a Santa behind that door. Or, there still could be presents. The flour footsteps next to Trevor's bare feet could have just been Daddy's. He might have gotten up to pee. Or worse, stepped out in the night to retrieve the presents Trevor wasn't supposed to know about, in which case the closet would be empty, as empty as the magic he'd wished existed.

Slowly, Trevor backed away from the closet. He stared for a long, thoughtful moment, his insides pulling him in two directions.

Working up the courage, he opened his mouth rather than the door. "Santa?" he whispered. And then, slightly louder, "Santa Claus?"

No answer.

He waited longer.

Still no answer.

This didn't mean Santa wasn't in there. He could have been hiding, waiting for Trevor to leave. But he knew… he knew the closet was empty. No Santa. No magic.

His chin quivered as he fought the urge to cry. "It's okay, Santa." A tear trickled down his cheek. "I won't tell." He wiped his nose. "I know you're in there. But I won't tell."

He spun and crept back to his bedroom, smudging the flour footsteps beneath his bare feet. In his room, he dropped his flashlight onto his dresser, collapsed into bed, and buried his head into his pillow.

Donny waited a good few minutes before he opened the closet door, a switchblade still in his grip. Surveying the darkened hallway, the black-jacketed teenager stepped forward, careful this time not to kick the stupid jingle bells that had lined the floor.

Glancing down the hallway, he spotted the lopsided purse sitting on a narrow table. He rummaged the purse and found cash and jewelry and loaded his small fanny pack. Donny knew better than to bring anything bigger than his trusty fanny pack when robbing these upper middle-class houses. Just enough to get by without alarming these rich dweebs.

A sigh from the bedroom at the end of the hall alerted him. He froze.

He remained a statue, listening.

Nothing for long moment, then another sigh—it must have been that kid who was talking to him through the closet door. The noise came from the cracked open door further down the hall. Donny crept forward for the door. He peered in. A skinny kid in reindeer pajamas lay face-down, one leg dangling off one side. He moved to leave, when the kid mumbled, "No... no, there *is* a Santa. There is…"

The innocence of the boy's words awakened something deep and warm within Donny. Something he hadn't considered since he'd been a scrawny punk himself a decade back. The mocking laughter of friends telling him there was no Santa ignited a flame within. His boyhood tears gave way to fists, which gave his classmate a bloodied lip and Donny another trip to the principal's office.

Instincts told him to leave. He'd already been there too long and there were at least another few houses he planned on hitting before sunrise. Yet, the pull to the boy felt stronger.

He took a heavy breath and stepped into the room.

"Good morning, sweetie," Mommy said as she shook Trevor awake.

The boy arched his back and struggled to open his eyes. "Mommy?"

"It's Christmas morning."

Trevor's eyes popped open. He sat up. "Did Santa come?" But the moment the words left him, he recalled last night—his call to the closet with no response, his sad walk back to bed.

"Of course. C'mon." She stood and stepped for the door. She stopped, looking down. "How'd flour get in your room?"

Trevor remained silent.

Mommy frowned at the messy floor, then left the room.

Trevor wanted to race out to the Christmas tree, but sadness weighing inside held him back. Even if there were presents, he knew they probably weren't from Santa.

He stood next to his bed and glanced at his dresser where his Batman flashlight lay on its side. He moved for the door, but something next to the flashlight caught his eye—a folded piece of paper beneath a pencil.

He picked up the paper, opened it, and read. His heart leapt with joy. He wanted to share the letter with everyone, but he knew nobody, not even his parents, would have understood. He tucked the letter into his drawer, and throughout that day and every Christmas day for years to come, he recited every word in his heart:

Hey, Kid.

Thanks for not opening the closet door. That would have spoiled the magic.

Your pal, Santa.

The Visit

Volume 3

The Visit

John Hope

I stood in the sanitized hallway of Saint Anthony's Children Hospital just outside the cancer ward, my head throbbed, and my body trembled at the thought: facing those children would crumble me. At fifty-two, I was decades older than the kids behind those white double doors. Yet, the power of their innocent faces was too much for me. I couldn't believe I let my agent talk me into this with a cheap bottle of Merlot.

Plastic ivy dotted with red berries and paper kid-made wreaths decorated the cancer ward's door, all superficial reminders of the fast-approaching Christmas season. At home, I no longer decorated for Christmas. No tree. No stockings. No nativity scenes. No Johnny Mathias. If the sight of children beyond this ward's threshold didn't make me fall to my knees, the additional decorations inside this room would.

I spun, poised to leave, when Jeannie, the perky nurse who coordinated this visit, appeared out of nowhere. "Ms. Springfield! Thank you for coming. The kids barely slept a wink last night."

"Um, yeah." I fidgeted.

She urged me forward with a hand on my back. "Come."

We emerged through the doors into a long, stanch room. The sun shone brightly from windows at the far end where a Christmas tree stood, adorn in sloppy paper ornaments. A blunt table near the doors was cluttered in coloring pages and crayons. A half-dozen beds lined each side of the room, each with a child perched and hugging one of my Dragon

Lure books. Some had Book One, others Book Two or Three. Their lively eyes and shiny scalps made them look like life-sized, hairless baby dolls. A few had Santa hats covering their baldness.

I crept forward behind Jeannie's springy trot.

"Look who arrived, boys and girls. Your favorite author, Ms. Sandra Springfield."

The kids bounced and clapped.

"They're all yours, Ms. Springfield." Jeannie ducked to the side, leaving me alone to face the troops.

My throat tightened. "Uh, hello. I—" Cold flushed over me. I locked eyes with the little boy at the end. His floppy hair, bright green eyes, squeezable rounded cheeks. For a second, I swore it was Charlie, my boy. "Um…I…"

"Why don't you tell them," Jeannie jumped in, "how you thought of your exciting book series?"

"Well…" I began, my mind scrambling like confused ants. I swallowed. "Yes, um. You see my son, Charlie. He loved dragons. We'd go the library, and that's all he wanted to read. And he knew them all. Hydra. The Amphithere. The Wyvern. The Lindworm. He'd pin his drawings on every wall."

A little girl bounced and held out a drawing.

"Look at my dragon!"

"And mine!"

"Yes, yes. They're very nice."

I blinked, and in my mind I saw Charlie lying on his belly at the center of his bedroom. Crayons and paper spread everywhere. He looked up and smiled. "Check out my Wyvern, Mommy!"

"Lovely." I knelt next to him, rubbing his back and bald head.

"He's scary but gentle. The only dragon who can dislodge emeralds with his diamond tail without damaging the jewel's magic."

"That so?" I was the fantasy writer, but Charlie always knew more than me. I caressed his smooth head, a reminder of the pain he suffered with every dose of chemo. Over time I watched him grow thinner, weaker, my beautiful flower wilting in the harsh sunlight.

I blinked. I was back in the cancer ward, a dozen kids smiling, shifting on their beds. My stomach twisted, knowing the pain they've suffered, the weathering path they were on.

A hand shot up.

"Um… yes?"

"When's the fourth book coming out?"

"Well, I'm not done writing it."

"When will you be done?"

"Um… I don't know." I hadn't written a word in years. Not since…

Christmas morning, wrapped packages glistening around the tree. I crept excitedly into Charlie's room. He lay peacefully, quiet. I touched his side. Cold. I whispered at first, then screamed. I rocked his limp body in my arms, shaking, angry at the world, tears streaming down my face and onto his.

After my Charlie was gone, I entered his bedroom, the bed unmade, hand-drawn dragons everywhere, Crayons scattered. The laughter of children outside, playing with their new Christmas toys contrasted the noiseless house where I stood alone. The quiet house stripped away every word, syllable, and story from my soul.

Now, here in the hospital, a dozen kids stared, their faces hungry for the unwritten book that lay sleeping in my abandoned imaginary world.

"It takes," I started, "a long time to write a book."

A little girl raised a hand. "Will you finish in a

month?"

"Uh…"

"Because," she continued, "my last round of chemo is this month. And my doctor said…" She looked down. "There won't be another." By the time she lifted her head, tears glistened.

A tide swept over the kids. Their smiles, their bounce, their excitement—gone.

I felt their loss, their pain and helplessness, mirrored in Charlie's eyes that grew foggy and distant in his last days. I was too late, for Charlie and these kids. By the time I complete the book, sell it to the publisher, and get it in print, some of these kids may be—gone.

Silence pervaded the room. Even Jeannie, still in the corner, said nothing, though her face pleaded. Seconds ticked, tears filled little eyes.

Suddenly, something inside me snapped. I leapt forward. My shoes slapped the tiled floor. "Listen!"

The kids gasped.

I said, "Everyone, close your eyes. Close them."

One-by-one, every pair of eyes shut.

"Now, picture in your mind, a cave."

A kid opened his eyes. "A cave?"

"Eyes closed!"

He shut them.

"A dark cave, giant stalactites dangling from above. A fog rolls in, surrounding you on all sides, and with it comes a foreign scent. You hear a sound, deep, menacing. You spin. A giant figure stands before you, three stories high. With an orange glow cutting through its sharp teeth, you know this giant Amphithere Dragon. Purple. Wings tipped with red claws."

"Draconia!" a girl called.

"Yes. Our beloved Draconia. She steps forward. You're afraid at first. But there's a pained look in her eyes. Someone has left her. Someone has broken her heart. Without words, with a mere weary droop of her blue eyes, you know, you can hear in your mind a cry for help. A cry to help her... find the love who... has left her."

The boy from the back asked, "Is this the next book?"

"Yes." I smiled. "And you're going to write it."

The kids reopened their eyes with smiles and mouths hung open.

"Us?" a girl asked.

"Yes! Each one of you pictured yourselves in the cave, alone with Draconia. She needs your help to rescue her loved one, to combat the evil forces of the Lindworms. To outrun the dragon hunters in every realm."

"When do we—"

"Now." I dashed for the stack of paper sitting on a small table near the room's entrance. "Here. Take some paper. Grab a crayon. Draw. Write. Continue this adventure before it's too late, for Draconia's sake… and your own."

The children sprang from their beds. They grabbed a couple pages and returned to their beds. They laughed and smiled and shared ideas and stories and scenes and heroes and villains.

I encouraged each kid as I skirted from bed to bed. After several minutes, I sank toward the doors. Jeannie touched my arm. I turned.

Her eyes glassed. "You truly brought joy to these kids." She breathed. "You don't know how… how much they needed this." She faced the kids. "How much they needed an escape from, you know."

I nodded and glanced at the kids. I knew their stories were illusions, fantasies, distractions from real life. Their treatments would continue. Their conditions may worsen. Yet, I sensed a truth I had somehow forgotten. "These illusions have the power of healing." I pushed at the door.

"You leaving now?"

I nodded. "It's time for *me* to write." I paused. "And maybe do a little decorating." I patted her arm, smiled warmly at the children, and walked down the hospital corridor, now with a lighter heart.

Story 7
Pass It On

John's Shorts
short stories - volume 2

Pass It On

John Hope

Christmas Eve.

Larry's history of suicide attempts left reddened, glazed slash marks down his left arm. He failed at everything, even suicide. He stroked the pocketknife that had tattooed his scars.

He once overheard a pothead neighbor explain the best way to kill yourself was to slice the veins lengthwise, from the hand to the upper arm. That way the blood wouldn't clot as easily. Larry sat in a wooden rocker and stared at his scars. His mind weaved around these darkened thoughts like a kid wandering the forbidden adult movie section of a video store, lusting over what may exist on the other side.

The mad honk of cars outside his apartment window derailed his thoughts. He hated this place. The fluctuating city noises, many of whom were likely last-minute Christmas shoppers, annoyed the hell out of him.

A grandfather clock ticked on the far wall – the only consistency in his life. He wound the clock every morning. It ticked its life away during the day, reminding him of the clutter that filled his life. Appointments. Doctors. Unemployment offices. Today, his final interview in an hour. Final because he decided it would be his last. Like everything else, he'd failed to get a job. His therapist warned him that if he wasn't actively looking, they'd take him away – lock him in a room, in a building, even worse than the hell he was in now.

Tick, tick, tick.

"Shut up, clock," he muttered, pressing knuckles

to his forehead.

It had been two months since his last day at work. Two long, torturous months since he'd been paid, since he felt like somebody. He was a working man. Work made him happy, fulfilled, and content – even if these feelings were temporary, even if the bad thoughts returned by the end of the day. Work was the only hope he had.

Tick, tick, tick.

Larry sneered and stood. His pocketknife clanked against the rocker. He turned and picked up the knife, shiny metal with a small red cross. He shook with guilt when he bought it several years back, hoping the cashier couldn't read his mind. He'd bought it for one reason.

He closed his eyes and squeezed the knife in his palm, still feeling the thrill of knowing he possessed the very weapon that would end his life.

He knew this last interview would fail. Why would it not? But there was no way he was going to return that useless therapist and tell him he still hadn't landed a job.

With his eyes closed, he pictured Benning Park. He saw the rusted bench near the giant oak. An isolated section of the park. He loved the area. That was where he would die. He had decided to die there on several occasions, but never made it out there. This time, he would slice his arm. And he'd do it in his favorite spot in the entire world. He felt ready. He wasn't going to fail again.

Taking a final look at the knife, he dropped it into his pocket. On his way out the door, he picked up the final copy of his resume he had printed. The interview was just a formality. Suicide was the goal.

A caterwaul of distant voices echoed down the apartment hallway. Aged, chipping paint on both sides of him, Larry tried to breath as little as possible. He often gagged on the smell of rotten cat feces leaching from the water-warped doors of the other low-income tenants.

He turned the corner and made a beeline for the closed elevator doors. He slapped the button and waited for it to arrive.

Movement in a shadowy corner forced him to jerk back.

A little girl no more than five whimpered in the corner next to an old shopping cart that had been there since he moved in. She clutched an expensive-looking doll, new with a pretty dress and hair, strangely matching the girl's. She was barefoot and her hair a little matted, but otherwise well-dressed.

It struck Larry how out of place this girl appeared. Most kids he'd seen coming in and out of his apparent were a dirt poor as he was. Little girls were often dressed in boy shorts and Budweiser T-shirts.

Nevertheless, Larry ignored her - at least he tried. He pressed the already lit elevator down button again with added force.

Her high-pitch sniffling pulled Larry from the elevator. He eyed her again, trying to be subtle. The girl reminded him of his older sister, Candice, who had OD'd on heroin a few years ago in the back of a boyfriend's van – the boy who used to beat her. Larry loved Candice. More than once, she'd been the only friend he had. He recalled laying in the front yard with her as kids, both looking up at the night stars and dreaming about life beyond their trailer park. Her wild, unkempt hair tickled the side of his face with each quiet whoosh of a nightly breeze.

The little girl next to him swiped a hand across her snotty face. Teardrops tapped against the wooden floor between distant city sounds.

The phrases, "Why are you here?" and "Why are you crying?" and "Where's your mom?" slipped in and out of Larry's head, never reaching his mouth.

Larry squatted.

She pulled in her legs and stiffened, still sniffling.

He stared for a long moment.

The longer he stared, the less tense she appeared.

At last, Larry spoke up. "You're lost."

Slowly, she nodded. Her arms wrapped around her folded knees, pressed against her chest. The admission of being lost caused her to wrinkle her forehead and cry harder than before.

He nodded, whispering, "It's okay. We'll find your mom."

The elevator dinged and the doors opened. Empty.

He said, "You live here?"

She shook her head, taking another snot swipe of her face.

"I didn't think so."

The elevator doors started to close but he stuck out his scarred arm and stopped it. Holding out his other hand, he said, "C'mon."

She didn't move.

"Don't be scared. I won't harm you." He paused. "We'll find your mommy. C'mon."

Shaking, she reached out her hand and gripped

one of Larry's fingers.

Larry stood, assisting the little girl to her feet. "That's it," he coached. "We'll find your mommy." He stepped toward the elevator.

The girl trundled her bare feet, barely walking, body shivering. The shadows on her face made her teary face look like an old lady.

The rickety elevator seemed to sway with Larry's weight. He tensed, hoping this didn't frighten the little girl. She stepped aboard, still shuffling forward.

The doors closed. Larry tapped the button for the first floor. The elevator shuttered with the frightening whine of the motors.

The girl squeezed Larry's hand with both of hers.

With the closeness and the small, enclosed space, Larry smelled urine, likely coming from the girl.

The entire descent felt long and stressed. Larry took shallow breaths and so did his small companion. Both stared at the silvery elevator door, etched with choice words and phrases that wouldn't be found in the Bible.

The floor shuddered. The girl yelped, pressing her body into Larry's leg. With a whine that sounded like wringing out a cat, the doors opened.

Slightly fresher, smoggy air wafted in.

Larry tapped the girl's rat nest hair. "C'mon." He stepped forward.

The girl shuffled along.

Two black men in Spandex and tank tops laughed and slapped each other next to a hall of postboxes. They stopped and eyed the pair.

Larry kept his focus forward toward the double glass doors leading to the city streets.

The girl stared at the men, wide-eyed, face red.

Outside, a wind flapped the girl's dress.

The sudden early winter chill nipped Larry's ears and he worried for the girl, shoeless.

But strangely, she appeared slightly happier. Not smiling, but no longer taxed with a deathly look of fright.

Larry tugged her hand.

She looked up.

"Does this look familiar?"

But the second the words left his lips, a giant smile grew on the little girl's face.

Larry twisted around.

Down the sidewalk, a short woman holding a pair of shoes and a small jacket sobbed, staring across the street.

"Mommy!"

Despite the rumble of cars, honking horns, and clank of metal on metal construction site noises, the woman spun and spotted the little girl. "Angela!"

The woman ran to her. She pulled her away from Larry, embracing the little girl. Both cried. "Oh, God, Angela. I thought... Oh, I'm so happy you're okay." She eyed Larry.

"Uh..." Larry let out a quick cough. "Found her next to the elevator. Fifth floor." He jerked a thumb at the building.

"Fifth?" She looked to her girl. "How'd you get on the fifth floor?"

"I... I..." she stuttered. "I don't know."

The mom looked to Larry. "You–"

"Stacy..." The little girl started, holding up her doll. Her bottom lip trembled. "... Stacy wanted to see the high building." Tears fell. "I got pushed out of the elevator. And I couldn't find..." Her crying overcame her.

The woman shook her head as she wrapped the girl in her jacket. She got to her knees and wiggled on one shoe, then the other. She shook her head. "I swear, sometimes. You're going to be the death of me. Wandering off. How many times have I told you? Stay by my side."

"Sorry, Mommy."

The mom's face and voice softened. "I know." She swiped a thumb against the girl's cheek.

Standing, the woman looked at Larry. "I don't know how to thank you."

Larry gave her a crooked smile. "It was nothing, Mommy."

"Please, call me Pam." She held out her hand. A purse that had been dangling from one arm slipped down. She pushed it up.

Larry shook her hand. "Take good care of her, Pam." He looked down at her. "I have to be leaving now."

The little girl pressed her body into Pam's leg. "Bye, Mister."

"Bye, Angela." Larry stepped away.

~~~

Pam watched Larry as she patted her daughter's frazzled hair.

Angela looked up. "Am I getting a whupping?"

Pam breathed and brushed the sides of her face, now raw with wiping away so many tears. "Not today." She shook her head. "I just don't know what I'm going to do with you. I thought you were dead or..."

"Or what?"

"I was just worried." She took another breath. The angel that rescued her daughter was already out of sight. Dozens of strangers walked, hobbled, and zigzagged up and down the city sidewalk. Cars zipped past, coughing out exhaust. "C'mon." She tugged Angela's hand.

As they walked, Pam reflected. Moments ago, thoughts of kidnapping, getting hit by a car, and various gruesome images flooded her mind. At one point, she recalled a photo she had stumbled across on the internet of a dismembered child's body, a bloody bucket, and the eyes of a sadistic serial killer. In utter helplessness, she even screamed at the passing cars, as if that would have brought back her little girl. The vacuum of her loss gave her insane thoughts, like throwing her body into oncoming traffic.

But now, with Angela's small hand in hers, such thoughts were distant and unreal. She had lost Angela. But, now, they were together. Safe.

They stopped at the crosswalk, waiting for the light to change. Angela looked up and smiled. The look always melted Pam's heart. She patted her hand, then kissed her forehead.

Pam took a deep breath and sighed. Despite her spinning head, she felt calm. She hadn't felt this peace for quite a long time. Any worries she might have had earlier this morning – the laundry, commitments, her job – gone. Now, it was just her and her little girl.

"Mommy, where's the car?"

Interrupted from her blissful train of thought, Pam hesitated.

"Mommy…"

"Oh, I don't…" She looked around. So preoccupied by the morning's potential catastrophe, she hadn't been paying attention where they were walking. "When I couldn't find you, I asked Jones to drive around and look for you." She paused and looked at the passing traffic. "Now, I haven't a clue where…"

"What, Mommy?"

An idea sprang to mind. Smiling, she took both of Angela's hands. "Hey, you wanna go to the park?"

She smiled. "Yeah!"

Pam looked up. "Let's take a cab there." Cab rides were rare and Pam knew her daughter regarded them as more of an amusement park ride than a mode of transportation. To Angela, riding in their limo was the norm.

Angela giggled. "Yeah."

Still holding on with one hand, Pam hailed an approaching cab with the other.

The cab squeaked to a stop. Pam opened the back door and urged Angela inside. Pam sat next to her, closed the door, and joined in with her daughter's excited giggle.

The cabbie peered at them through the rearview mirror.

She pulled Angela's seatbelt across her lap and clicked it other end. "To the park, please. Benning."

"Benning? That's only a few blocks. Sure you don't want to walk?"

She smiled. "No. We're treating ourselves to a cab ride."

The cabbie nodded and pulled the cab from the curb. He looked at the two through the mirror. "You two seem excited."

"Yes we are…uh…" She leaned to read the driver's credentials. "… Harona."

"That's Harone. Something going on at the park?"

"No, we're just…" Pam wrapped an arm across

Angela's shoulders. "… enjoying life."

Harone nodded and gave them a crooked-tooth smile.

Pam noticed a photo attached to the bottom of Harone's credentials. In it, he stood in a dark room with his arm draped over the shoulders of an elderly woman, both smiling.

Pam smiled. "Is that your mother?"

Harone nodded at the photo and looked to the rearview mirror. "How'd you guess?"

"Oh, we mothers have a knack." She gave Angela a squeeze.

Harone nodded. "Actually, I still hadn't bought her a Christmas present yet."

"It's Christmas Eve."

He shrugged. "Yeah, I know."

"You better not forget. Moms don't like that."

"I know, I know." Harone leaned to the side, checking his blind spot before merging to the next lane. "Actually, she really wants this old phonograph she saw in an antique store a couple blocks from here. Problem is, stuff like that is a bit much for my paycheck."

Pam placed a hand on one cheek. "Oh, I love those things."

"She had one like it when she dated my father. The two used to sit on the couch and listen to Bing Crosby, Perry Como, Billie Holiday." He rubbed his nose.

Pam said, "Your father's passed?"

Harone nodded. "I suspect the phonograph brings her back to those days."

Pam touched her cheek. "That's so sweet." She patted Harone's shoulder from the backseat. "Maybe an angel will give you a hand."

Harone snorted. "Yeah, maybe. A big, fat maybe."

The cab squeaked to stop at the park's entrance. Harone tapped the lighted monitor attached to dashboard. It read, $6.55.

Angela unbuckled and pulled at the door's handle.

Pam said, "Slow down, Angela. I have to pay the man." She fumbled through her purse. "I don't want to lose you again."

Angela opened the car door and jumped out, but kept a tight grip on the door. She swayed side to side. "C'mon, Mommy."

"Okay, okay." She pulled out a bill and handed to Harone. "Thanks, Harone." With the bill sandwiched between their hands, she gave his hand a squeeze. "And don't forget your mother." She winked.

"Never."

~~~

She stepped out and closed the door behind her.

Harone clicked the meter and at last noticed the bill in his hand. He frowned. Waving through the closed windows, he called out, "Madam! Madam!"

But mother and daughter had already dashed into the park.

He looked at the bill again. One hundred dollars for a fare less than seven bucks. He rubbed it between his fingers to ensure its authenticity. The lady's words came to mind. 'Maybe an angel will give you a hand.' He shook his head. "Wow." Such random acts of kindness were rare in his business.

When he was boy, he had shined shoes in New York's Grand Central Station. He imagined the sweet smell of the polish even today, so many years later. The wooden shoe shining throne-like chairs, throwbacks from the 1920s, were typically manned by old, hunched men with long stories and quick hands. Harone had neither. Businessmen often kicked and cursed him, all feverishly eager to get to work and make their millions. Until one man came along. He whistled a song and shared anecdotes with Harone and by the end of the shine he didn't care that Harone had left a scuffmark here or there. Rather than cash, the man flipped the boy a single coin and tapped his way down the giant, echoing hall with an umbrella in hand. Harone later pawned the rare coin for $85 the next day. That had been the biggest tip he'd ever gotten in life, until now.

Feeling giddy, he turned off the dome cab light and drove off. He technically wasn't supposed to clock off this early, but his hand burned with the hundred dollar bill, and he had to act on it.

A few miles later, Harone pulled up to Russell's Antiques and parked. Stepping out, he shoved the bill into his pocket and entered the store.

A man in a pinstriped suit stood opposite a woman in a gray business dress and an old man in a hand-knit sweater. The three stopped talking and turned to Harone.

The sudden silence and three pairs of eyes bearing down on him halted Harone at the door. The musty smells of antiques mixed with a waft of freshly polished display cases and Windex.

The old man bounced forward toward him.

"Please, please. Come in." He grabbed Harone's hand, shaking. "Hello. May I help you find anything?"

The old man's hand felt wrinkled and clammy. Harone slipped his hand out of the man's tight grip and gave a short cough before speaking. "Uh, yeah. My mom was in earlier and was looking at an old phonograph. You don't still have…"

The old man's eyes brightened. "Yes." the old man thought, "Eva Homsi, was it?"

Surprised, he asked, "What?"

"Your mother, Eva Homsi?"

"Uh, yes. That's her name."

"Oh, lovely lady. I know just the one you mean." He shuffled over to a dark corner of the store.

Harone followed.

The man rattled off words like a giddy cartoon character. "It's right over here. Excellent condition. You know your mother sure knows her phonographs. This is a rare one. Ah, here it is. Look at that solid wood. They don't make 'em like this anymore, you know."

Unsure what to think about this old man, Harone kept his distance. He nodded.

But seeing the antique up close, thoughts of his

mother trumped the old man's strangeness. He imagined the look on her face when he showed up at her door with the gift. The soft look in her eyes. The tears.

The man rattled off more details, but Harone barely listened. He stuck a hand in his pocket and looked for a price tag on the phonograph. "Uh, how much?"

"Oh, how much?" The old man unexpectedly peered toward the man and woman near the cash register, both of whom glared emotionless. "Uh, well…" The old man's eyes bounced until they found Harone's face. "How does two thousand sound to you, young man?"

Harone's heart sank. He crunched the hundred-dollar bill in his pocket. It suddenly didn't feel like much of tip anymore. He swallowed. "Oh." He felt like an idiot. He knew his mom yearned for this antique. But that's all he knew. He hadn't a clue how much it cost.

The old man perked up. "Oh, but I'm willing to bargain." His forced smile and pleading eyes had an unexpected look of desperation.

Harone was used to seeing similar strained looks in his fares when they were caught in traffic and were desperate to be wherever they needed to be. He saw sweat beading in his gray and white receding hairline. "Um… but I'm not even close."

The old man clapped his hands. "Oh, but, uh… Well, how much do you have?"

Rather thrown off by the old man's forwardness, he balked. "Well…actually…" He was never much of a bargainer, not like his father. But he knew never to tell the seller how much you had to spend. Yet, there was something sincere in the old man's face, something that cracked open the truth. "A hundred."

The old man nodded with a smile. "A hundred it is. Sold." He closed the top of the phonograph and busily moved aside smaller trinkets around it.

Harone scratched the side of his face, baffled at what just happened. "Is that hundred including tax?"

"Uh…" He looked up at me. "Yes, yes. One hundred even. I'll cover sales tax for you."

The younger woman stepped forward, her heels clicking against the floor. "I'll get it, Daddy." She tapped the man on his shoulder. "You ring him up."

"Oh, okay." The old man skipped to the register.

Harone followed.

Once he paid, the woman stepped to the counter

with the phonograph and rested next to Harone. She breathed, slightly winded from the antique's weight, and smiled at him. "Hope your mom enjoys it."

He nodded. "I know she will." Turning to the old man, he said, "I… I don't know how to thank you."

"No. No thanks needed. It's our pleasure. Please. Come again."

Harone picked up the hefty wooden box. He gave one last nod to the old man and the lady, and walked out the front door.

~~~

The second the door swung shut, the old man jumped. "Yippee!" He swung a hand in the air like a half-crazed school boy.

The man in the suit, Mr. Davis, frowned. He glared at the two. "Okay, fine. You win. You just bought yourself another month." He raised a single finger. "But just one month. Like I said before, if this place doesn't turn a profit…"

"I know, I know." The old man waved a hand in front of him like dispelling an odor.

"Mark my words." Mr. Davis mounted both hands on his hips. "I will close this place down."

"Yeah, yeah."

Mr. Davis stormed out, slamming the door

behind him. The little bell above the door that chimed the entrance of a customer snapped off and clank to the floor.

Rachel breathed. "We lucked out that time, Daddy."

"Luck?" The old man placed both hands on the counter. "Rachel, luck had nothing to do with it. Just you wait. I'll turn this store around. By next month, we'll be turning people away." With the sweep of a hand, he pantomimed shooing a crowd away. "May have to hire some help."

Rachel gave him a lop-sided frown. "I've heard that before." She crossed her arms. "You can't keeping making these insane bets with Mr. Davis forever." She shook her head.

Just moments ago, Mr. Davis, the owner, made a bet that if her father couldn't sell a single item in the next five minutes, he'd close the store for good. Less than five seconds later, a man appeared asking about a phonograph for his mother.

The old man stepped around the counter. "Before I couldn't keep up. But now... now after the operation, I'm fit as a fiddle." He tapped his shoes in an impromptu, Fred Astaire-like dance. "Ready to work long, hard hours. You just need a little optimism, that's all." He leaned in. "You're pessimistic, like your mother."

~~~

"Yeah, well…" she trailed off. Glancing at her watch, she gasped. "Oh, no. I'm late for… I've got to go."

Giving her father a light peck on his cheek, she picked up her briefcase and purse, rushed out the door, and haled a cab. A couple passed before one pulled over. She stepped in. "The Franklin Building, and hurry."

The cab sped off.

She snapped open her briefcase and shuffled through some paperwork. She fished out her planner and read off the name of her next interviewee. She rubbed the side of her face, trying to transition her mind to work mode, but her father invaded her thoughts.

Rachel had heard her father's optimism speech dozens and dozens of times before. But this time strangely, she had finally heard him. Almost a year ago, she lost her pessimistic mother to cancer. And just two months ago, she had nearly lost him, her father, the only man she truly loved in her life. Painful memories bubbled up. The nights in the hospital, the evenings sitting alone on her back porch. The prospect of going back to that loneliness frightened her. Part of her knew it was inevitable. Nobody lives forever. Still, maybe she could try a little optimism. Try to be as fool-hearted as her father had always been.

The cab had lurched to the side and stopped. She blinked and snapped her briefcase close. "Why not, Daddy?" she whispered. "Why not?"

Rachel pulled cash from her purse, paid the cabby, and stepped out. She rode the elevator up to her office. With every ding of the elevator, she imagined her father's register dinging another sale. She closed her eyes and envisioned handing Mr. Davis another rent check, seeing him scowl in frustration. She always enjoyed ticking him off.

Somehow, this daydream made her feel a little better, a little lighter. She felt different, more confident than she had felt in a very long time. She whispered, "So this is what optimism feels like." She laughed and tapped her shoes together, a strange habit she had done as a kid any time she was about to do something crazy. "Okay, Daddy." She shook her head. "Okay." She looked up and took a deep breath. "If you can turn that shabby store around, then maybe I can smile every once in a while."

The elevator doors opened. She strode toward her office.

Swinging around the corner, she passed her secretary. "Sally, send in the first candidate." She continued onto her office.

~~~

Sally nodded to Larry, sitting in the line of chairs opposite her desk. "You're up."

He stood slowly and walked into Rachel's office, closing the door behind him.

Several minutes later, the door opened. Larry walked out with an unexpected smile, head high, and dropped his silvery pocketknife into Sally's trashcan.

About the Author

John Hope is an award-winning short story, children's book, middle grade fiction, young adult, and historical fiction writer. His work appears in science fiction/fantasy anthologies and multiple collections of the best of the Florida Writers Association, amongst others that'd bore you to mention. Mr. Hope, a native Floridian, loves to travel and play board games with his wife and kids. He enjoys long-distance running and his wobbly legs have transported him nearly 40,000 miles through forests, deserts, swampland, snow, and other unreasonable terrain. Some have their suspicions that he is part alien, while others are sure of it.

Read more at www.johnhopewriting.com.

More by John Hope

Silencing Sharks
Deaf and bullied, 13-year-old Peter discovers he alone can talk to sharks. And he must put this unique skill to use to rescue them from poachers, while surviving neighborhood bullies and saving his blackmailed dad from getting fired.

Father's Violin
Trapped between armed Soviet and American soldiers in post WW2 Berlin, 13-year-old Hertz uses the only thing he has left from his father: a violin. Armed with this instrument, Hertz, his best friend Jakub from Poland, and sister Elsa maneuver through the city's underground, inspiring hope through music.

Secret Adventures of Foxfire: Fixing Walls
Secret Adventures of Foxfire: Busting Walls, a coming of age tale of boy forced to survive his step-dad and neighborhood bullies, escaping into his bedroom to draw an exciting adventure of secret agent Foxfire. Book contains illustrations of comic Foxfire and tips on being a secret agent.

No Good
12-year-old Johnny "No Good" and his newly adopted brother find themselves in the middle of a manhunt for a small town murderer when No Good learns the other is connected to the prime suspect. This captivating story, set in the 1940s Sanford, Florida, taps at the heart of a boy struggling to understand himself and brotherhood in the midst of southern racism.

Fairy Tales, the Sequel

Whatever happened after *happily ever after*? This thrilling collection of classic fairy tales answers the question, each story going deeper into the fanciful creations the world has loved and shared over the centuries..

Pankyland Series (Books 1, 2, and 3)

Three-book series with 11-year-old Panky, his little brother and pals, and a crazy theme park.

Pankyland

When Panky loses his little brother at a theme park, he's forced to team up with his rival to find the boy before his parents find out.

Pankyland 2: The Movie

Panky and younger brother Craig get the chance of a lifetime: starring in Pankyland the Movie. But fate takes a turn for the worse when a jealous parent kidnaps the brothers after her kid doesn't get the envied role.

Pankyland 3: Be Little World

After Be Little World opens and steals away Pankyland's guests, preteen heroes discover a conspiracy. Amongst spats and a rap battle,the kids attempt to bring culprits to justice.

Colby in the Crosshairs

After Colby's estranged father returns to his white trash home, the 9-year-old struggles to survive a promiscuous neighborhood mother, money sharks, and an uncontrollable autistic older brother while discovering the true cost of living and brotherhood.

Go show kindness to someone.